Table of Contents

Pug Puppies   3

Photo Glossary   15

Index   16

About the Author   16

rourkeeducationalmedia.com

Can you find these words?

cuddle

eyes

puppies

tail

What do Pug puppies look like?

eyes

They have big **eyes**.

They have a curly **tail**.

What do Pug puppies act like?

They like to explore.

They like to be lazy.

They like to **cuddle**.

They need exercise.
They like to go on walks.

Did you find these words?

They like to **cuddle**.

They have big **eyes**.

These are Pug **puppies**!

They have a curly **tail**.

Photo Glossary

cuddle (KUDH-uhl): Holding something closely in your arms with love.

eyes (eyez): The pair of organs used to see with.

puppies (PUHP-eez): Dogs that are young and not fully grown.

tail (tayl): Part of an animal that sticks out at the back end.

Index

big 5
curly 6
exercise 13
explore 9
lazy 10
walks 13

About the Author

Hailey Scragg is a writer from Ohio. She loves all puppies, especially her puppy, Abe! She likes taking him on long walks in the park.

© 2020 Rourke Educational Media

All rights reserved. No part of this book may be reproduced or utilized in any form or by any means, electronic or mechanical including photocopying, recording, or by any information storage and retrieval system without permission in writing from the publisher.

www.rourkeeducationalmedia.com

PHOTO CREDITS: cover: ©Sasha FoxWalters, ©manley099 (bone); back cover: ©grase (inset), ©Naddiya (pattern); pages 2, 3, 14, 15: ©Liliya Kulianionall; pages 2, 4-5, 14, 15: ©Natalia Fedosova; pages 2, 6-7, 14, 15: ©Irina Stdyarova; pages 8-9: ©morrowlight; pages 2, 10-11, 14, 15: ©Irishka1; pages 12-13: ©Alice and Kuba Potocki

Edited by: Kim Thompson
Cover and interior design by: Janine Fisher

Library of Congress PCN Data
Pug Puppies / Hailey Scragg
(Top Puppies)
ISBN 978-1-73162-876-3 (hard cover)(alk. paper)
ISBN 978-1-73162-875-6 (soft cover)
ISBN 978-1-73162-877-0 (e-Book)
ISBN 978-1-73163-346-0 (ePub)
Library of Congress Control Number: 2019945799

Printed in the United States of America,
North Mankato, Minnesota